As Fast As You Can

written by Pam Holden
illustrated by Kelvin Hawley

I can run as fast as you can.

I can jump as high as you can.

I can yell as loud as you can.

I can hit as far as you can.

I can dig as deep as you can.

I can whisper as quietly as you can.

I can blow as hard as you can.

Pop!